The Tutor:
A Ghost Story

Rod Galindo

v2.0

Wordwraith Books

ISBN-13: 978-0-9908743-6-2
ISBN-10: 0990874362

Wordwraith Books, LLC
705-B SE Melody Lane #147
Lee's Summit, MO 64063
www.wordwraiths.com
@Wordwraiths

Cover art by The Cover Collection
www.thecovercollection.com

Rod Galindo's website www.rodgalindo.com
Rod Galindo's Twitter @RodAGalindo

This story is dedicated to my tireless editor, Jeni Frontera. Your spreadsheet of literary magazines that we utilized to submit our short stories eventually led me to the "New York City Midnight Short Story Challenge." Were it not for that contest, the brave little Max and the beautiful Claire would never exist.

Thank you for checking out my short story, I hope you enjoy it!

Allow me to send you the first three chapters from my upcoming novel,
Distress Call.
Simply hop over to RodWerks.net/SecretSC and tell me where to send it! ☺

For more information on upcoming projects and books, please visit RodGalindo.com

The Tutor:
A Ghost Story

"Max, look at number seventeen again."

"Why? What's wrong with it?"

Claire fell silent.

He looked again. "Oh. I always do that!" He ground the eraser into the paper.

"Easy, you'll leave a pink smudge!"

Max corrected his mistake and slammed his pencil onto the desk. "Why can't I remember this stuff? Why is it so easy for you?"

"I don't know. I've just always been good at math. When I was your age I won a math bee."

"Really? They had math bees back then?"

"Oh of course! We even had words for our carts and buggies." Claire gave him a sideways look.

"That's not what I meant! I'm sorry, please don't get mad at me."

"Don't worry, Max, I'm only teasing. I could never be mad at you. Okay, next question."

"Can we take a break, please?" Max rubbed his head with both hands. "My brain hurts."

Claire chuckled. "Sure."

"Tell me another ghost story!"

"Oh Max, I think I've told you every one I know a dozen times now. Aren't you tired of hearing them?"

"Claire, I'll never get tired of your stories. But wait a minute!" He turned on the small lamp at his desk, bolted to the bedroom door, switched off the overhead light, and planted himself back in his chair in a flash. "Now I'm ready!"

"Okay. Which one do you want to hear tonight?"

"You pick."

"Alright." Claire cleared her throat and began in her prettiest voice. "Once there was a pretty red-headed girl who lived in an old house on—"

"Oh no, not this one!"

"You said I could pick."

"But this one's so sad!" He looked behind him at the now-darkened room. "And it scares me more than the others."

"Oh, but it's my favorite one, Max. And isn't that the whole point of a ghost story? To scare you?"

Max sighed. "Okaaay."

"Okay." Claire smiled and sat up straight. "Once there was a *beautiful* red-headed girl who lived in an old house on Hollow Street with her parents and her dog, Rex. On the property just over the creek lived the boy of her sixteen-year-old dreams. She had never known a time without him. They went to school together, they rode horses together, they shared their first kiss together…"

"Ugh, can we skip the mushy parts this time?"

Claire tilted her head. "Someday you might not mind so much."

"Yeah well that 'someday' is not today."

"Fine."

Truth be told, she was right; Max didn't mind the mushy stuff anymore. But of course he couldn't tell her that.

"So one bright summer day, she met him out by the stables. She had bad news. 'We have to move,' she told him. 'In two weeks. My father's job is moving him to Baltimore.' 'As in Massachusetts?' the boy asked without looking up. 'I guess,' the girl replied.

"It's Maryland." Max rolled his eyes.

"Yes, you're very smart, Max, now hush. She didn't know where Baltimore was, but she knew she didn't want to go. 'I hope we can spend more time together between now and then,' she told the boy, 'I might not ever see you again.' He still didn't look at her. He just brushed his horse with more vigor."

Max took a cracker from the plate his mother had left on his desk. Nibbling helped to calm his nerves during stories like *this one.*

"'Don't be mad,' she pleaded," Claire continued. "'I don't want our last days together to be full of anger.' 'I'm not mad,' the boy replied, and grabbed her arms really hard and pulled her to him. The girl told him he was hurting her, and he immediately quit squeezing, but she never forgot how violent he could be. 'I'm sorry, I didn't mean to hurt you,' he lied. 'I'm just so mad! I would do anything if it meant you didn't have to leave. *Anything.*'"

"I hate that guy," Max whispered, narrowing his eyes.

"Then he kissed her," said Claire, closing her eyes.

Max saw her peek before continuing, but he pretended not to notice, instead focusing on the cracker.

"He kissed her so gently it made her toes curl and her hair stand on end. He had the most wonderful kisses in the world. Each one made her forget the hurt."

Max cleared his throat.

Claire sighed. "The girl spent every day with him, and cried every night." Here Claire opened her eyes fully and stared into Max's. "Until her last day finally came."

Max nibbled faster.

She stood from the small bench and sauntered around the desk. "'Today's my last day here,' she told the boy at the fence between their properties. Neither said a word for a long time. The boy finally asked, 'Can I come over tonight and see you? Just us? One last time?' 'Sure!' the girl exclaimed, and was so, *so* happy she would get to spend one last eve alone with him."

Max shifted in his seat, and ate the rest of his cracker whole. He looked around the room. The corners of his bedroom were almost black. Four human-like turtles stared back at him from the far wall, their faces twisted in anticipation of a fight, ninja-style weapons at the ready. Lightning flashed outside his window, and the wind picked up. *Maybe I should have left the light on?*

Max turned back to see Claire smiling at him. "What?" A delicate sound of thunder rolled in the distance. He stuffed two crackers in his mouth at once and rubbed his sweaty palms.

Claire bent over the desk and leaned in close, continuing the story in a whisper. "That night, a sound outside startled her. She put down the book she had been reading— *Alice's Adventures in Wonderland,* her favorite—turned off her bedside lamp, and crept slowly towards the half-open window. The curtains billowed gently in the breeze. The faint scent of the elderberry bush her father planted for *supposed* medicinal purposes wafted inside. The snap of a twig froze her in her tracks."

Max could not help but gasp, even though he'd heard the story a dozen times.

"Was it her lover?" Claire asked rhetorically. "A burglar? The bogie man?"

"Oh please, we both know it's not the *boogie man,*" Max said, his nerves calming a bit. He took a drink to get rid of the cotton-mouth that too many crackers in a row does to a person.

"Who's telling this story?"

Max swallowed the last of the water and set the empty glass on the desk without a sound.

"I'll never get over the funny way children say 'boh-gie' these days," said Claire.

"Anyway, you're right, it was indeed the boy!"

Max rolled his eyes.

"She was so happy to see him! He ever-so-quietly climbed in through the window and hugged her warmly." Claire drew her arms to her chest and spun once, coming to a stop in middle of the large rug in the center of the room. "'I have to tell you something,' her lover said. And then his head snapped toward the bedroom door. The girl, afraid, did the same." Claire also jerked her head in the direction of Max's bedroom door, exactly as her characters did in her story. "'Did you hear something?' she asked the boy. 'My father may have awoken—' He pulled her closer, interrupting her train of thought. 'Sweetheart,' the boy said, 'I have found a way to keep you here. I got the idea from William. You don't have to leave, we can be together. Forever.' 'Really?' the girl replied. 'How? Who's William?' Then the boy set his palm firmly in the center of her back, and stared into her wide, green eyes. 'A poet. And a friend.' He put his soft, wet lips to her ear. 'Trust me,' he whispered. 'I trust you,' she replied, barely even hearing her own voice. Then his lips met hers once again. This one, this kiss… oh, it was a terribly passionate kiss. The best one yet. The best one ever. Light. Feathery. Tender. His touch was absolutely—"

"Mushyyy!" Max held the last syllable long enough to remind her.

Claire took a deep breath. "You can *really* ruin a beautiful moment, you know that, Max?" She gave him a look that would kill most boys where they stood.

Max slumped in his chair. *Please calm down. Please calm down.*

She closed her eyes.

Please, please, please…

"She lost herself in that kiss," Claire continued, eyes still closed. "She lost everything in that one, glorious moment. And then something pierced her heart. It was cold. Like *ice*." Claire opened her eyes wide. "The girl's eyes shot open, and she screeeeeamed."

Max was ready. He smashed his sweaty palms to his ears as hard as he could, but it barely helped. Claire let out her signature high-pitched banshee howl, the one that always turned Max's toes into fists and raised the goosebumps all over his body. But this one was different. Max had never heard her let loose like this before. The scream went on and on, and made the empty glass on his desk sing all by itself. Claire was really putting on a show for him tonight! Her mouth finally closed, and the soul-stealing scream died away. Max's hands shook when he released the death-grip he had on his own head.

Claire went on. "'I love you,' the boy told the girl. She went limp. He lowered her to the floor. She lay there, staring at the open window. A tangy, coppery scent replaced the sweet smell of elderberries. The room spun as her vision began to fade. A moment later, her One True Love collapsed upon her, his face next to hers. A bloody kitchen knife clanged on the wooden floor and came to rest just out of reach. The girl couldn't move. 'I will love you forever,' he whispered. And then, everything went black."

Max heard footsteps outside his bedroom door. Someone was roaring his way. His heart pounded in his throat. Muffled voices reached his ears. *What are they saying?*

He made fists to stop his quivering fingers. He looked at Claire and waited.

She seemed nonplussed, ignoring the footsteps and the voices. She wasn't finished.

This wasn't the end of the story.

"Then," Claire said, "to her great surprise, the girl woke up! She wasn't alive, but she wasn't entirely dead, either. She was alone. Alone in that big, old, creaky house." She turned her head and stared out the window. "She never saw the boy again. Nor her parents. She saw Rex though, and he saw her. And they played together often, until the little dog finally died. Then they played less often. And eventually, the girl was completely alone."

Max's eyes usually teared up at this point, but they didn't tonight. His eyes flashed between Claire and the bedroom door. The muffled voices had stopped.

"To this day, the girl still roams the halls of that old house on Hollow Street, searching for her lost love. For the boy who made sure she *never* left that house. The boy who *murdered* her…"

The footsteps outside resumed their stomping. Coming closer. Claire had turned, her entire body now fixated on Max's bedroom door.

He swallowed hard, and prepared himself for anything that might come through—

The door flung open wide. Max jumped out of his skin and nearly fell out of the chair. He stared, mouth agape, at the pale figure looming before him in the doorway.

"Max, is everything alright in here? *Max! Are you okay?*"

He somehow found the strength to breathe again. His shoulders slumped. "Yes, Mom. I'm fine."

Max's mother looked around the room. "Why is it so dark in here? Are you finished with your homework? Did you hear that just now?"

"Hear what?"

"Come on, you can't tell me you didn't hear that scream!"

Max and Claire both shook their heads at the same time.

"Don't play games, now."

"I'm not! It was probably my dumb sister."

"Sophie said it wasn't her, I asked." His mother crossed her arms. "That girl and her room, I swear…"

"Maybe it was the storm?" Max suggested.

Mom cocked her head. "Not even tornadoes sound like *that*."

Max looked at Claire. Claire looked at Max. They turned to look at the woman in the doorway.

"Oh, nevermind!" Mom finally said. "Your dad's probably watching some silly horror movie downstairs again!" She shook her head. "That ridiculous stereo system of his! Don't worry, I'll make sure he turns it down. He knows you're doing your homework, I don't know why he has to have it *so* loud! Are you about finished?"

Max turned and glanced at his book. "Yeah, I only have a couple more questions."

"Good, it's after eight thirty. I want you in bed on time tonight, mister. Do you hear me?"

"Yes, Mommm." Another brief flash of lighting filled the room.

Max's mother turned to leave, then paused. "So weird, though. It sounded like the scream came from just down the hall, not downstairs. You honestly didn't hear it?"

"I didn't hear anything," Max said. He looked at Claire, who shrugged her shoulders.

The woman rolled her eyes. "Whatever, okay." Gentle thunder answered the lightning bolt that lit the room few seconds ago. "Oh, Max! I got your Spiderman jammies washed. They're in your dresser there."

Claire giggled.

"Mom!" Max jumped up and grabbed the doorknob.

"Alright, alright, I'm leaving."

He slammed the door shut.

"You make sure to brush your teeth!" his mother called from the hall. "And turn on a light! I don't know how you can possibly see in the dark!"

"Okay!" Max rested his head on the closed door.

"She can't help it," Claire said. "She loves you, that's all."

"Yeah, yeah." Max looked up. His head and shoulders cast a dark shadow on the white door in the lamplight. "You want to play shadow puppets?"

"Okay." Claire said, and appeared beside him.

Max backed away from the door and dropped to his knees to give them more "canvas space" on the door and wall. He intertwined his thumbs the way his father did. An eagle appeared on the wall next to the door.

"So majestic!" his tutor announced.

He made a dog. "Arf, arf!"

Claire smiled and pretended to pet it. "Good puppy!"

Max put his palms together and curled up one index finger. He clapped his hands in rapid succession. "I'm-a-gonna eat you up!" he growled.

"Oh no!" Claire exclaimed. "Don't let that nasty old alligator eat me!" Her red pony tail bobbed from side to side and she raised her hands to protect her beautiful face. "Help me, Max!"

"I'll save you, fair maiden!" He made a dramatic gesture and killed the foul beast.

"Yay! You saved me! The kingdom is safe once again!"

Max smiled at Claire. She was at her loveliest when she smiled, too. And she usually did. But at times she could be terrifying.

"You have such a great imagination, Max," she said. "You can even make something as simple as shadow puppets entertaining!"

Max's smile turned tight-lipped. He looked down at the large rug in the center of the room. Directly underneath was the dark brown spot on the hardwood floor that no one could remove. His gaze then wandered to the dark red stain on Claire's flowery nightgown. He looked up, into those green eyes he was so very fond of. "I only wish you could cast a shadow, too."

Claire: The Tutor's Ghost Stories

Twelve haunting tales document Claire's experiences in the old house on Hollow Street, spanning 200 years.

"The Tutor" is included, in addition to eleven new stories, to make a complete collection of Claire's paranormal adventures.

Recommended for ages 13 and up.

Available now on Amazon.com!

Please enjoy this early excerpt from
Claire: The Tutor's Ghost Stories

A New Family

"Haunted?" the realtor asked, her voice carrying from the parlor. "Oh no, don't be silly, Mrs. Newsom! I mean if you want to believe in such delly in this day and age you can, but I don't, that's for sure!"

Claire scoffed. *That's a lie if I ever heard one.*

Throughout the tour of the old house on Hollow Street, Claire had been able to see the realtor plain as day, which meant the woman believed in ghosts as much as Claire believed in dogs. She sat on the landing of the grand stair, watching and listening with little interest as the blonde in the gaudy purple dress finished her tour. The three intruders lollygagged into the foyer and stopped not far from her.

"It's Miss Sawyer," said the tiny brunette. With her short bob, she looked more Claire's own age than someone old enough to be shopping for houses with her husband.

The realtor blinked, her blonde beehive swaying. "I'm sorry, what was that?"

"We're not married," the male half of the couple explained.

Not married? But you're—

"Oh! I'm sorry," said the realtor. "I simply assumed—"

"It's okay," said Miss Sawyer with a big grin, "that will all change in a couple of weeks!"

The realtor's face lit up. "You're getting married! Congratulat-ee-o!"

"Thank you!" squealed the young woman. "I'm so excite-sees I can't stand it!"

"You don't believe the stories are true, do you?" asked the young man of the couple, who didn't look excited at all.

"Oh, of course not," replied the realtor. "These old, gothic houses from the Nineteenth Century have so much history, and so many people have lived in them, there are bound to be all kinds of cray-zee-zay-ney tales from that time period! Back when common, viggy folk were much less sophisticated and educated in the ways of science."

This lady and her slang! Claire rolled her eyes. *And I thought Max and his sister spoke funny back in the late Twentieth Century!*

The blonde stopped in the center of the foyer and turned to face the young couple. "Alright, if there are no more questions, everything looks fabu-lo-sees from what I can see. Mr. Newsom, if you'll press your thumb here, here and, um, let's see... here."

"Oki-dayo," he said in a perky tone.

"Oh and read over this last part carefully," the realtor said, and pointed to something on the transparent device she had just handed over. "Make sure everything in the purchase agreement is accurate."

Claire watched the man study the thing in his hand. Why this lady would print something as important as house-buying paperwork on a pane of glass was beyond Claire. *All he has to do is drop it and poof! No more agreement! Idiots.*

"This will go into the housing database immediately?" asked Mr. Newsom.

"As soon as I have your thumbprint on the final line," the realtor said. "Speaking of which, when you're happy with everything, your last print goes right here."

Well that's stupid. Don't they know you can just wipe thumb prints off a piece of glass? These people are bonkers.

"While you're going over that, I'm going upstairs to visit the ladies' room. That's really the only thing bad about this house: only a single bathroom! But, you gotta admit, it's one awesomely-dawsomly powder room!"

"Biggest one I've ever seen in a house of this era!" said the brunette.

"Okiday-way," Mr. Newsom called after her, his gaze fixated the little rectangle in his hand.

Claire still hadn't decided if she could live with this couple if they did indeed buy the house. They seemed nice, if a little batty. If they proved otherwise, she knew a few tricks. They would leave soon enough, just like all the others she didn't care to have around.

The lady in purple trotted up the staircase, which now creaked here and there with age. Claire followed her. Not that she was afraid the realtor would steal anything in a once-again completely empty house, she simply didn't care for visitors she didn't know.

Once the realtor reached the top of the stairs, she started talking out loud. "Charlie? It's me. I'm closing on the house now, so I should be home in an hour. Make sure you pick up Benji from school today— what?" A pause. "No! You know how I feel about that new nanny! She's complete moodisauce!" Another pause. "I know you just reset her memory but she needs her prime motivator flashed for sure, if not replaced altogether!" She stopped walking for a moment and stared straight ahead, pursing her lips and narrowing her eyes.

Claire walked around in front of her and studied her face, head, shoulders and sleeves. *She must be talking on a telephone of some kind, but where is it?*

"Charlie, you get the old one back! I mean it! I'll de-ex her! Oh yes, I will! I didn't have any trouble turning in the last one! If you don't—" She barreled forward, right through Claire. "Oh my!" The woman halted and shivered.

Claire shook all over and flicked her hands, as if flinging off a revolting liquid. "Eww, yuck!" she said aloud.

The woman spun around and looked from side to side, then focused on points further down the long hallway.

Claire stared her down.

"No, no, it's okay," said the realtor, "I thought I heard something. Whew! Brrr! I wigged a really bad draft just now! I should have worn hose today." She turned back around and made her way toward the bath. "Anyway, we'll talk about the nanny situation later. Just *please* pick up Benji today? Please-ies? Thank you, Charlie." There was another pause, after which her voice turned to a whisper. "Yes! Hold on, let me get into the bathroom!"

This piqued Claire's interest. When the bathroom door closed, Claire closed her eyes, and blinked herself inside.

"Okay, I can talk now." The lady in purple continued in a whisper. "Yes it was the last thing they asked. Well what do you *think* I said? I made it sound like it was all silly-billy-bay to ask such a thing!" The lady raised her skirt and dropped a set of frilly panties.

Claire had never seen the likes of them, nor wanted to. She turned her back.

As the woman did her business and continued to babble to herself, Claire moved over toward the double-sink and stared into the oversized mirror. She frowned. *Oh my! What a rat's nest!* She ran her fingers through her red mop in an attempt to untangle the mess. *Ugh! I should have tried to steal a hairbrush years ago, when I had the chance!* She shook her head back and forth, which always built body and fluffed her mane up like a lion. She bit the inside of her lip. *That's not good enough. I can make it much bigger than that!* She bent over and performed the fluffing ritual once more.

Behind her, the lady in purple continued. "Remember those stories the old man in the diner told me about the haunted places around town? Well I did some Googling. Get this. I told you about the teenage girl who was supposedly killed in this house, right?"

Claire stopped shaking her head and listened.

"Well, apparently it's true. And after her father found her dead on her bedroom floor, he took one of his hunting rifles and drove or rode or whatever down to the old Branton house and— Hmm?"

She held her breath, still bent over, not wanting to miss a word.

"Oh you know, the smaller, one-story ranch that backs up to this property. You remember, I drove you by it a while back. Any-hoos, so this Harvey fellow kicks open the door and, without a word, puffs out the boy's daddy-o. Cold blood. Right in front of the mum." The realtor finished up and flushed the toilet.

Claire realized then her mouth hung open like a fly trap, and shut it. *Father? You did what?*

"Well, yeah, klaa, of course they did," the realtor continued. "The judge reduced the sentence though. Called it a crime of passion after just losing his daughter and everything. But he still got Murder Two. Twenty years. Yeah they were lolly-lo lenient back then! But that was what, a hundred and sixty years ago? Give or take?" A pause. "Oh I don't know, the website didn't say. Disappeared into history."

Claire stood up straight, and closed her eyes. *Oh, Daddy. Why?*

"Her mother went on to marry a railroad tycoon. Used the whole tragedy to her advantage, sounds like. Totes votted a millionaire!"

Could it be true? Had her family fallen completely apart after her death? If so, it was little wonder she'd never seen hide nor hair of her parents! They'd never made it to Baltimore. At least her Father hadn't; he'd been locked up after avenging her death! Claire heard the lady turn on the faucet.

"Well no, a million dollars is nega-notts today, but back then it was like a trillion! Believe me, he was rich in his time."

And you, Mother! Claire wasn't surprised her mother hadn't waited for Father to be released from prison. She had run off with another man to try to forget. And one even richer in order to maintain her lavish lifestyle. *But could I blame her? What would I have done?*

"You know the Claire Marie clothing line?" continued the woman. "Yep! That's her! Named it after her dead little—"

The realtor's voice cut off abruptly. Claire opened her eyes. The woman was staring directly at her in the mirror.

Uh oh.

The bubbling blonde had distracted her with all the talk of her family. Claire had lost her concentration, her focus that allowed her to remain invisible. And since the lady was already screaming bloody murder at the top of her lungs, it was much too late to do anything about it now.

But honestly, have I really gotten that ugly that you have to scream so? I mean, most of my skin is still attached to my bones!

The lady whirled around to face Claire. She stopped squealing, and her eyes darted about, apparently searching for what she had just seen in the mirror. Then she spun back around, locked eyes with Claire's reflection once more, and started in again. Even louder this time.

"Oh come on!" Claire protested. "A lot of a hundred-and sixty-year-olds are missing their noses! And an eye or two."

The woman's arms flailed about, but her feet seemed glued to the floor.

Well, might as well have a little fun at this point... Claire took a deep breath, and levitated herself off the ground. She raised her arms, extended hooked, bony fingers, and bared every one of her not-pearly whites with as much ferocity as she could muster. Her hair and bloody nightgown billowed about in a wind that came from another plane. How the room always darkened when she did this, Claire had not a clue. But she thought it was really— and here she stole another word Max and his sister had liked to use so much—*cool*. She stared at herself in the mirror, concentrated, and tried to make her eye holes glow this time.

The realtor backed up to the sink, her face a twisted mess.

"Hey! Your beehive's blocking my view!" Claire shouted, but she was pretty sure it came out as nothing more than a banshee howl in the living world, considering the decomposed state of her vocal cords.

The woman melted to the floor, her screams degenerating to whoops and gasps. Lightning flashed around the room, surprising even Claire. *Wow, didn't know I could do that!*

The realtor scrambled to the door on all fours. Her fingers fumbled for the ancient doorknob, but her fingers didn't seem to work.

Claire floated up behind her.

The blonde stopped fumbling for the door, and she slowly peered over her shoulder.

Claire leaned close to her ear. "Boo."

One last "Aaaaaaahhh!" spewed from the realtor's throat right before the door flew open. The terrified woman fell in the middle of the hallway in her haste. She looked like one of Max's Saturday morning cartoon characters trying to take off, her arms and legs sprawling all about, her dainty heels longing to find enough friction on the hardwood floor with which to launch her body to safety.

Claire chuckled to herself. *This is kinda fun. No wonder Sophie hated me back then!*

The lady in purple all but tumbled down the stairs to the landing, still releasing little whoops and gasps as she tore down the smaller flight of stairs to the foyer.

Claire returned to her normal human self. The lightning, darkness, and wind died away. She wisped invisible and blinked to the landing.

"Sandy, are you okay?" Mr. Newsom asked.

The realtor hyperventilated her answer as the young man helped her steady herself. "I'm fine! I'm fine! Just fine! Um, my house! My husband rang. Yes! My stove was left on! My kitchen's on fire!"

"What?"

"On fire?" repeated Miss Sawyer.

"Yes!" shouted the realtor, dropping the rectangle of glass with the glowing symbols in her haste. To Claire's surprise, it didn't break. "I have to go!"

The brunette shook her head. "But how could such a thing even happen?"

"I don't know! My housebot! It's on the fritz-o again! I have to go!"

The man scooped up the glass device from the floor. "Sandy! Don't forget your Googlie!"

The realtor stopped in her tracks, spun on her toes, snatched the rectangle from Newsom's hand, and bolted out the front door. She didn't even bother to close it behind her.

Mr. Newsom called after her. "So you'll call if there's any issues, right?"

There was no reply.

I hope you enjoyed this teaser of *Claire*

Available now on Amazon.com

Dear reader,

I hope you enjoyed "The Tutor." May I ask a favor? I would be thrilled if you could hop over to Amazon.com and post a super quick review. Good or bad, either is fine; like I've often said, an honest review is better than a glazed donut any day!

Also, I entertain all cool sci fi and speculative fiction ideas. e-mail me! rod@rodwerks.net

A little teaser: In my upcoming, heart-wrenching tale, **"Distress Call"**, Rae Marshall—a young hero not unlike Claire—fights fear, hunger, and an icy death in an attempt to save herself and her little sister from a doomed transport vessel, while the captain of a rescue ship races against time itself to save them.

Visit RodWerks.net/SecretSC to obtain a free download of the first fifteen pages! ☺

Rod Galindo
July 2016

About the Author

Rod A. Galindo arrived on Earth in the Spring of 1970. He's been trying to stay out of trouble ever since, but has now accepted that finding it is one of the three things he does well, right behind drawing and right ahead of spelling. He's beamed all around the world thanks to various military and government positions, but proudly calls Kansas City home. Mainly because his request for transfer to Stargate Command was denied. AGAIN.

"Major Galindo" has nearly thirty years of service under his belt in the U. S. Army, both Active Duty (as an enlisted M-1A1 Abrams tank crewman, Operation Desert Storm) and the Kansas Army National Guard (as a Field Artillery officer, Operation Noble Eagle and Operation Iraqi Freedom).

"Rod Galindo" is a worn-out father of four; two cyber-smart boys aged 15 and 12, one German Army (Bundeswehr) Soldatin who is as dangerously clever as she is beautiful, and he fills in as full-time father to a special young lady who never really had a dad to call her own.

Rod is a fully assimilated and very active member of the Wordwraiths Writing Collective and Wordwraith Books, LLC (learn more about our authors and books at Wordwraiths.com). Enjoy his shiny art or delve into his literary musings at RodWerks.net or RodGalindo.com.

www.ingramcontent.com/pod-product-compliance
Lightning Source LLC
Chambersburg PA
CBHW020611130626
46552CB00007B/3149